BRAVE

Parents' Magazine Press • New York

JOHNNY O'HARE

by Eleanor B. Heady

pictures by Steven Kellogg

To my mother for her love of verse

Many of the animals mentioned in this story can be found only in Australia. The koala bear is small, with gray fur, and carries its young in a pouch, just as the kangaroo does. The dingo is a yellow-brown, wild dog, and the kookaburra is a bird whose call sounds like laughing.

A billabong is the Australian name for a pool of water left standing when a river runs dry or changes its course. The water is still and murky, and here the crocodile swims. The koala bear and the kookaburra often make their homes in the tall gum trees along the banks.

The Bunyip is a mythical creature of Aboriginal lore, and stories are told of him throughout Australia. No one has ever seen the Bunyip. But everyone agrees that he lives under the waters of the billabong, coming out only at night to roam the countryside.

Johnny O'Hare
Lives way down there
In the upside-down land
of koala bear.
He isn't afraid of anything,
Or so he says. "Not anything!

"I'm brave," says Johnny,
"As brave can be.
There isn't a thing can frighten me!"

Johnny goes out
To the sheep shearers' camp

Where the men tell stories
That may be true,
Those old dark wise men
From long ago
Tell the stories their grandfathers knew,

Those shivery tales
Of the time of dreams
And mystic magic,
Those make-believe tales
Of days that are gone.
They tell of a creature who came at night
Up from the water,
Slippery and long,
Who slithered out in the chilly air
Up from the murky billabong.
And Johnny listens,
Brave Johnny O'Hare,
While the old men tell of the Bunyip there:

"The Bunyip was slimy
With scales of black,
And a row of spines
Down his snaky back.

"And he rushed about
In the dark of the moon,
Wailing a chilling, shivery tune.
Now if you should hear him,
Beware, beware!
That Bunyip scared everyone, everywhere!

"That's the way we heard it
From long ago.
Maybe the tales are true,
We don't know."

"Ha, ha, ha," laughs Johnny O'Hare.
"I'm not afraid,
I don't care,
I don't think the Bunyip's there.

"A just-pretend thing
Can't give me a scare.
You're fooling me, sure,"
Says brave Johnny O'Hare.
"If the Bunyip is real
He can't catch me,
For I'm as brave as brave can be."

Johnny O'Hare
Who lives down there
In the land of the kangaroo,
Where water lies long
In the billabong

And trees droop gray
In the still, hot day,
Where dingoes howl and crocodiles lie
In warm, deep pools
Under summer sky,
Waiting for someone who may come by
To give them a meal or two,

Johnny goes out
That very day
To the billabong
Where he likes to play
In the shade of the gum trees
That line the bank
Of the muddy waters.
And he gives a shout,
"Oh, wicked Croc,
If you're about,
Show your ugly face,
Hey, come on out!"

Then the water ripples
And slowly parts,
As up from the surface
A spiny back,
Two beady eyes as black as black,
A horny tail and a spiky snout
Show brave Johnny O'Hare the Croc is about.
Then Johnny laughs,
"I'm not afraid.
Get back in the water,
You can't eat me."

But the kookaburra in the tall gum tree
Laughs and hoots, "Ha, ho, hee, hee,"
And the shy koala, looking out
From his leafy home,
Blinks his little eyes
And stares at Johnny in surprise.
"It's you again, Johnny O'Hare,"
Mutters the sleepy koala bear.
"Go on away, let us be.
You're very brave
As we can see."

Then lazy koala curls up tight,
Shading his eyes,
His back to the light
Goes to sleep high in the old gum tree.

But the crocodile watches Johnny O'Hare.
He sniffs to himself,
"Brave Johnny O'Hare,
He's safe as can be
On the billabong side.
But should he fall in,
I take great pride,
I could open my jaws
So very wide,
That with one snap and a swish of my tail
I'd grab that Johnny without fail.
Then what would he say, Brave Johnny O'Hare?"

But Johnny laughs
And throws a stone
That splashes close to the crocodile's snout.
"I dare you, Croc, to come on out!"
Yells Johnny O'Hare
From way down there,
Screeches Johnny O'Hare as he skips about.
Then the crocodile squirms
In his muddy hole.
"Oh nuisance and bother.
That boy will be
The very undoing and death of me.
He's the plague of my wicked crocodile soul,
That screeching, shouting Johnny O'Hare."

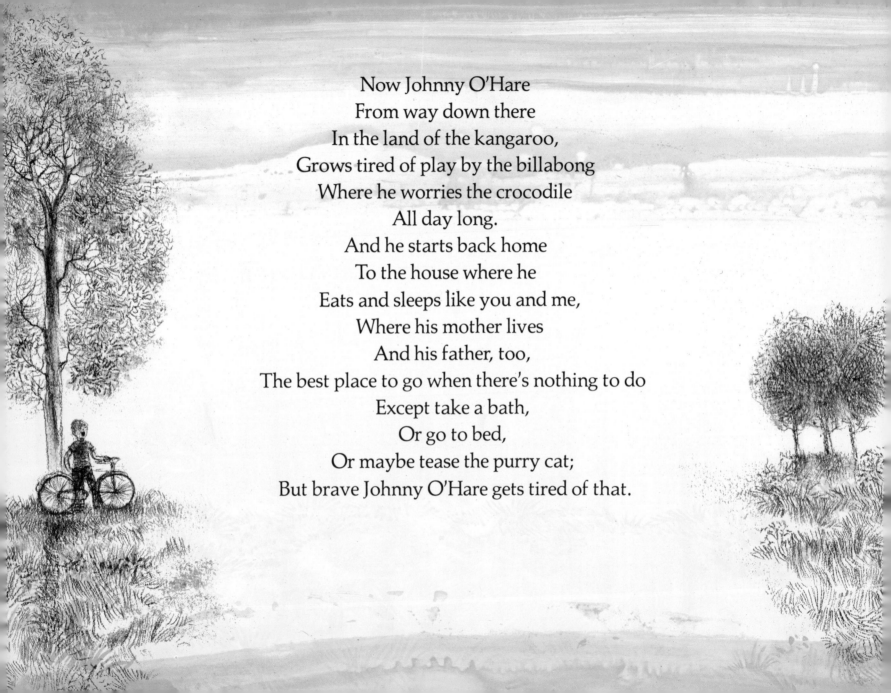

Now Johnny O'Hare
From way down there
In the land of the kangaroo,
Grows tired of play by the billabong
Where he worries the crocodile
All day long.
And he starts back home
To the house where he
Eats and sleeps like you and me,
Where his mother lives
And his father, too,
The best place to go when there's nothing to do
Except take a bath,
Or go to bed,
Or maybe tease the purry cat;
But brave Johnny O'Hare gets tired of that.

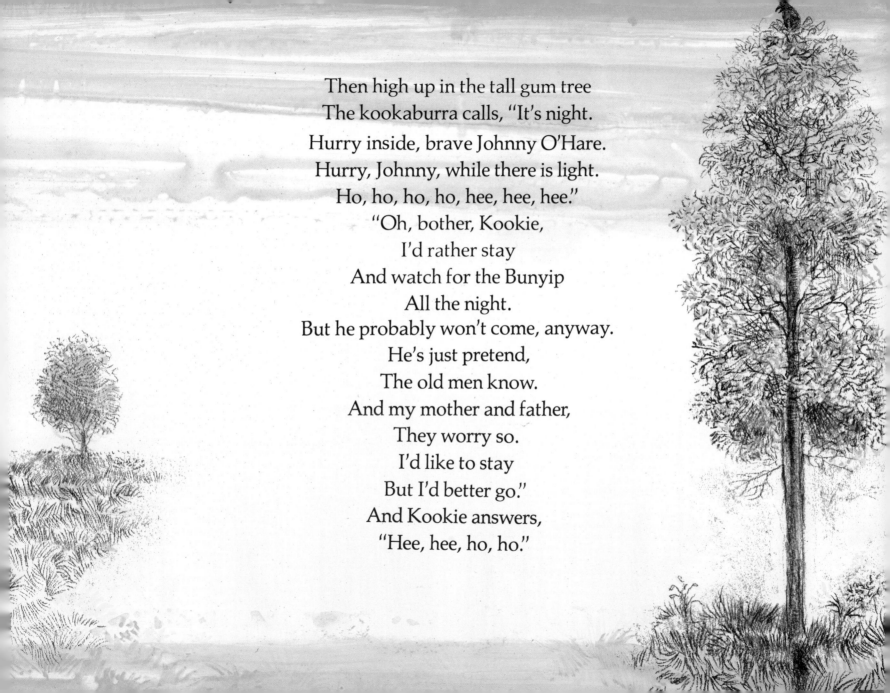

Then high up in the tall gum tree
The kookaburra calls, "It's night.
Hurry inside, brave Johnny O'Hare.
Hurry, Johnny, while there is light.
Ho, ho, ho, ho, hee, hee, hee."
"Oh, bother, Kookie,
I'd rather stay
And watch for the Bunyip
All the night.
But he probably won't come, anyway.
He's just pretend,
The old men know.
And my mother and father,
They worry so.
I'd like to stay
But I'd better go."
And Kookie answers,
"Hee, hee, ho, ho."

So he rushes home,
Brave Johnny O'Hare,
Hurries home in the fading light,
Back to his mother and father and
That very unfrightening, furry cat.

And Johnny O'Hare,
Brave Johnny O'Hare,
Tells of the Bunyip in the billabong.
"He can't give me the tiniest scare,
That make-believe thing in the billabong there.
I'm not afraid," says Johnny O'Hare.

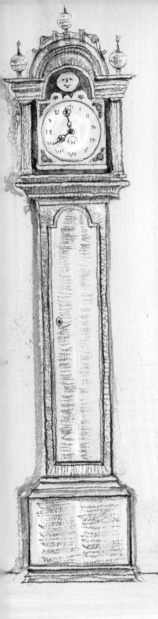

Then he yawns and squirms and says,
"I guess I'm a little sleepy.
I've had a day.
I'd like to go out,
But I'd better stay
And get some sleep.
Some other time I'll watch for the Bunyip.
He can't scare me,
For I'm as brave as brave can be,"
Says Johnny O'Hare
From way down there,
Yawns tired and sleepy Johnny O'Hare.

So off to bed goes Johnny O'Hare
To dream of the Bunyip in the billabong.
The dingoes howl a mournful song,
But Johnny O'Hare,
Sleepy Johnny O'Hare,
Doesn't hear them.
He doesn't care
How long they howl by the billabong there.

Then—plump! Right on top of Johnny O'Hare,
Something lands in a slithery heap
And Johnny jumps up,
A tremendous leap.

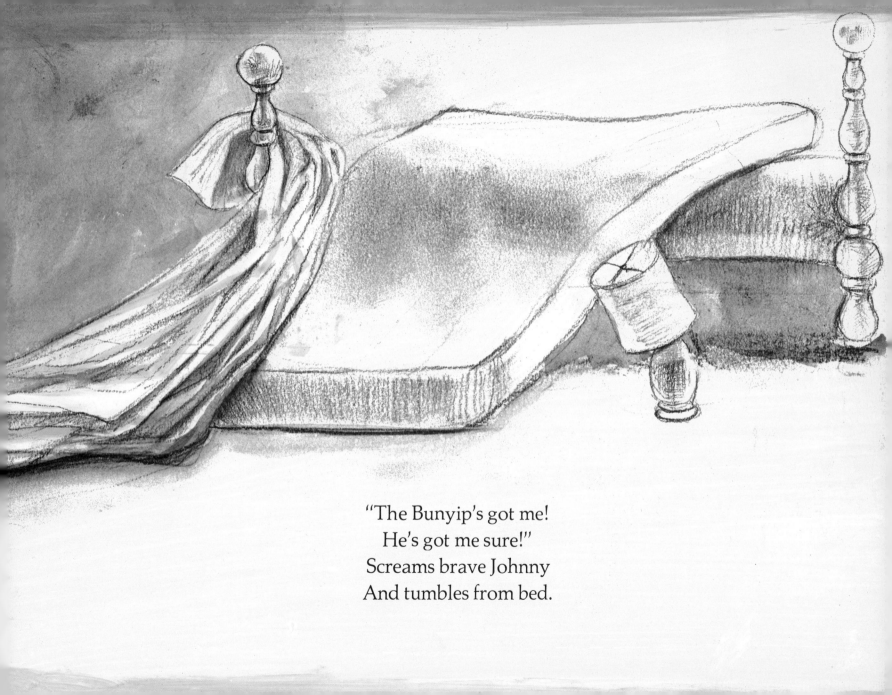

"The Bunyip's got me!
He's got me sure!"
Screams brave Johnny
And tumbles from bed.

What does he hear?
"Meow" and "Purr"
From that very unfrightening, furry cat.
And Johnny O'Hare is glad of that.
"I knew all the time
Those stories weren't true,"
Says brave Johnny O'Hare
From way down there
In the land of the kangaroo.

ELEANOR B. HEADY scribbled her first verses when she was a child on a ranch in southern Idaho. Recently her collection of East African folktales, *When the Stones Were Soft*, was selected as an Editor's Choice book for the year by *School Library Journal*. She is also the author of *Jambo Sangura* and *Coat of the Earth*.

Mrs. Heady has traveled around the world with her husband, a professor at the University of California. While he is engaged in research, she collects folktales and ideas for her stories. In Australia, she became fascinated with the tales of the Bunyip and with the character of the Australian people. *Brave Johnny O'Hare* is an outgrowth of that experience.

STEVEN KELLOGG, in addition to being an illustrator of children's books, is also well known for his etchings and drawings which are exhibited at galleries in New York and Washington, D.C. He has taught etching at American University in Washington.

He was the winner of the Pitney Bowes Scholarship award and also the Rhode Island School of Design European Honors Fellowship which made possible a year of study in Italy.

Mr. Kellogg lives in Sandy Hook, Connecticut with his wife and six children. Among the books he has illustrated for young readers are *Martha Matilda O'Toole*, *The Rotten Book* and *Gwot!*

1 - 3 grades

Date Due			
'JI 22 MY 17'91			
AG 21			
MAP 12			
MAY 11			
AUG 10			
AUG 1			
AG 14 '82			
MR 26 '83			
AG 5 '83			

Brave Johnny O'Hare